WERE-WOLVES and WILL-O-THE-WISPS

FRENCH TALES OF MACKINAC RETOLD

written and illustrated by
DIRK GRINGHUIS

MACKINAC ISLAND STATE PARK COMMISSION

MACKINAC ISLAND STATE PARK COMMISSION

Copyright 1974

Mackinac Island, Michigan 49757

Standard Book Number 911872-14-0

Printed by: Trikraft, Inc., Williamston, Michigan
1st Edition: 7,000 copies
2nd Printing 1980: 10,000 copies

WERE-WOLVES and WILL-O-THE-WISPS

CONTENTS

Dedicated to

René Chartrand and Brian Dunnigan, colleagues and close friends.

WERE-WOLVES AND WILL-O-THE-WISPS

1

On Mackinac Island French names abound. Andress, Archambault, Bazinaw, Bourisaw, Cadotte, Couchois, LaPine, Perault, St. Onge, Therrien, Vanier, are all descendents of the French voyageurs and fur traders who have called the Straits of Mackinac their home for over three hundred years.

French voyageurs first passed the Island of the Great Turtle in 1634. Beginning in the 1670's a small French community was established at St. Ignace on the mainland. In 1715, the fort and town moved south across the Straits where Fort Michilimackinac was erected. Until 1761, the French flag flew over the stockaded village. Here the sturdy voyageurs, who paddled the massive 35-foot canoes from Montreal, rendezvoused with the Indians from deep in the interior. Furs were exchanged for trade goods and rum and stories were told around the campfires on the beach.

During the long Mackinac winters, those hardy French families who wintered at the frozen Straits had many long hours to devote to story telling. Around a roaring fire, with the bitter wind blowing through the cracks in the bark-roofed log cabins, skilled *raconteurs* spun tales and legends which they had learned as children. These traditional tales, which originated in eastern Canada or even in France, were often given a local setting to make them more humorous or frightening. Sometimes the stories were told about actual people, but more often fictional names were used.

When the British military seized control of the Upper Great Lakes in 1761,most of the French *habitants* remained. In 1780, during the American Revolution the French community at Michilimackinac followed their church of Ste. Anne de Michilimackinac when it was moved over the ice to Mackinac Island. A new town was founded and the traditional French culture was maintained, though with a growing leaven of English Scots and later Irish. Until the end of the Fur Trade era in the 1830's the French Canadian voyageurs provided the muscle which moved the furs and freight. Hundreds of them gathered annually at Mackinac in the summer and the traditional tales were told and retold.

These canoemen who carried the tales into the upper Great Lakes and to Mackinac also loved to sing. More than entertainment, these songs set the pace for their flashing paddles on the long voyage into the *pays sauvage* or back country. Carrying trade goods for which they received rich furs from the Indians, they traveled long and hard, making as many as 36 portages carrying several bales weighing 90 pounds each. At night around the fire was the time for the French fiddle, two drummers beating on pans, and the men singing and dancing.

The songs too often appear to be overly sentimental, speaking of lost love or earlier events in the homeland. But these chosen are representative of several types and they tell us that the voyageurs for all of their reputation as tough brawlers and drinkers of brandy, were little different from simple pioneers of any land.

The tales, on the other hand, can be quite moving. Most here tell of the supernatural, of witches and goblins and werewolves. Stories to listen to in front of a fire, and then shiver deliciously under the covers, in fear all night.

Customs and costumes change, but the world of earlier centuries lives on in folklore.Tales, dances, songs, all remind us of simpler times, of entertainment passed down verbally through generations. Fortunately, much has been preserved and written down by such dedicated folklorists as the French Canadian, Marius Barbeau, Le Gaspé, and others.

As for sources, only the Indian's legends* originated in America. All others were brought over by the immigrants. Then later, new tales and songs were added in the New World.

French Canadian lore came, of course, from France; some songs unchanged for 300 to 400 years. And as is the case in Mother Goose, many of the original political overtones were completely unknown to the later singers.

Special tale tellers, called *raconteurs,* spun out tales, especially to the young. Many listeners were from five to sixteen. In turn they married and retold the stories and sang the old songs to their children and grandchildren.

In order to preserve this rich French heritage which has made such an impact on the Straits of Mackinac we are here presenting some typical tales and songs translated from the French. We trust you will enjoy their retelling as much now as when they were originally told at Mackinac.

*See *Lore of the Great Turtle. Indian Legends of Mackinac Retold,* Gringhuis, Mackinac Island State Park Commission

GOOD GOBLINS AND BAD

2

To the Voyageurs at Mackinac and other *habitants* or colon-
ists of French Canada the goblins were the best known
and the subject of many folk tales and superstitions. Their ori-
gin was in France and they were called *lutine* in the old Nor-
man language, which may mean a ghost, a white lady or a goblin. In Canada they were called *"lutin"*.

Interestingly enough, in the French Canadian lore, they
may be good or bad, all depending upon how well they are
treated. Tiny, full of mischief and fun, they might protect the
family and the household goods. Usually they were in the shape
of a dog, a cat, a bird, rabbit, rats, mice or even a small snake.

Black cats, usually thought of as bringing bad luck, were
considered the best of protecting goblins and no one would
even think of mistreating one or driving it from the home. To
have one in the barn or stable, or better still a whole family
was considered wonderful luck.

Of lesser power were white cats, rabbits and other household animals. It is said that once a small boy killed a slim yellow
snake in front of a farmer's house. The farmer rushed out waving a stick and gave the boy a sound thrashing. Later he told his
habitant friends that he would rather have lost his best horse
than the snake. It had lived in his cellar for many years and was
a good luck *lutin*.

His friends were sympathetic and all agreed that good *lutins* could bring fine weather for planting or harvesting, take care of the animals, help in the healing of the sick members of the family and even keep the milk from souring.

But to the unlucky or unwise who mistreated a *lutin*, bad luck was sure to follow. Then the cats or animals became vicious pranksters. When the *habitant* farmer awoke in the morning and tried to put on his pantaloons, he would find them sewed shut at the top and knee, there would be sugar in his porridge or salt in his tea, while his wooden shoes or *sabots*, or moccasins, if he was in the back country, would be filled with pebbles or dried peas. Nor did they stop there. The meat in his stew pot would be turned to stone, dishes broken, furniture upset and other damage. The stable also received its share of pranks. The favorite trick was to take revenge on the farmer's favorite horse. Every night for months, the evil *lutin* would braid and tangle the horse's mane and tail and cover the poor animal with burrs and thistles. Even worse were the nightly rides the goblin took, leaving the animals winded and useless the next day.

The only way to stop these antics was to use magic or religious objects. The sprinkling of salt sometimes terrified the goblins. Should this fail, the farmer as a last resort, might take one white and one black cat, kill and skin them and make lattice work strips from the black and white hides. These were placed over all windows and openings. This was said to keep out even the most terrible of the evil *lutins*. There were other methods which will be told later.

But best of all was the kindly treatment of these creatures. Then instead of ill, the family received good. Children were protected, young maidens were helped to find a husband. The *lutins* of French Canada never forgave an ill or forgot a good deed.

The next tale is about another kind of *lutin*.

6

THE MYSTERIOUS RIDER

3

Near the shores of the Straits of Mackinac beneath the shadow of the Fort, lived an old French *habitant*. His name was Jean Pierre La Bec *dit le formidable*. It was the custom to give nicknames such as this, which means "called the tremendous" which usually told some special trait or characteristic of the person. Often the name stuck, and in later years the *habitant's* descendents took over the nickname in place of the family one.

Jean Pierre was a great story teller or *raconteur*. The equal, some said, of Jacques, called the Long Bow. Often on winter evenings, the *habitants* near the fort, as they had done before in Montreal or Quebec, or on the surrounding farms, would gather in the house of the *raconteur*. There, in the evening, they would listen to the old tales told by a master story teller.

Filling his beloved pipe with *kinickinick* (Indian tobacco), he lighted it with a coal from the fireplace and began his story.

There was a young man, he said, named Louis, *dit le cavalier*, or horseman, who upon his father's death, inherited a fine farm at Grosse Pointe near Fort Detroit. The soil was good but instead of raising many crops, Louis preferred to raise grass for his horses. For in winter, his favorite sport was to race on the ice along the shores of the Lake. Riding high on the seat of his sled or *cariole*, he was wrapped warmly in an Indian trade blanket coat of bright red with a black stripe. The hood was drawn over his head and the whole tied at the waist with a bright sash of many colors. On his hands he wore gloves of wolf skin.

As he urged his little black Canadian pony on, you could hear his cries above the other racers. *"Avance donc, Caribou!"* Like a winter whirlwind he sped on past the others until steed and sleigh were only a speck on the ice.

At the end of the course was a tavern which served *liqueur de pêche*, a fiery peach brandy. As its fumes rose to his brain, Louis told amazing tales of the speed and the records broken by his beloved black Caribou. She could clear at a single bound, he claimed, cracks in the ice 20 feet across.

Every day Louis drove along the lake shore, his fine mare prancing as though all eyes were upon her.

One night with the rest of the habitants, he went to visit Antoine Griffard whose magical violin always sent feet tapping until the sun rose. It was dawn, when Louis made his way to the stable. As he went to harness Caribou, to his amazement he found her covered with foam, her mane tangled with burrs, her head drooping. Puzzled, Louis *dit le cavalier* said nothing to anyone but decided that the next time he made the long drive to and from the fiddlers, he would take a lesser horse.

But the next morning and the next he found poor Caribou exhausted and disheveled as though she had been driven at top speed the whole night through. That night he padlocked the door and scattered on the ground ashes so that he might discover footprints of the person who was tormenting him. Hurrying down in the morning he found the padlock still locked, no footprints, but Caribou again was exhausted and sweat-streaked.

Completely baffled, he at last went to an old man who was a great friend and told the terrible story.

The old man looked fearfully about and then in a hoarse whisper said, *"C'est Le Lutin qui la soigne"*, (it is a goblin who takes care of her).

This goblin or *lutin*, was a dreaded monster sometimes called *La bête a Cornes* or the horned monster, who delighted in riding near to death the favorite horses of *habitants* living in the area.

But *le Cavalier* only smiled, *"Non, mon ami,"* he said. "This is the work of someone jealous of my fine mare."

But the old man shook his head. "This is not just a story of *lutins* told to us at our mother's knee or by a *raconteur*. You must brand Caribou with the cross, or put a sacred medal around her neck. Only then will you be safe."

Dejected, Louis *dit le Cavalier,* returned home. He could not believe a goblin would bother him, he had done him no harm. And so he decided that night to watch and see what happened.

As soon as it was dark Louis stationed himself at his bedroom window. As the moon rose he could see the stable door clearly. Across his lap was a loaded musket. As he sat there quietly, an old rhyme told by his grandmére came back to him. It went:

> Hang up hooks and shears to scare
> Hence the hag that rides the mare
> Till they be all over wet
> With the mire and the sweat,
> This observed the manes will be,
> of your horses, all knot free.

Perhaps he should do as his old friend had said, and hang a saint's medal around Caribou's neck. But before he could move, he heard the frightened neighing of a horse. Then before his unbelieving eyes, he saw the barn doors swing open and his beloved Caribou, eyes rolling trembling all over, come flying out. And on her back, something strange, something as black as the mare's coat. The horse and rider steered straight for the path beneath his window. Louis raised the musket then let it fall, while his hands and knees began to tremble and sweat stood out on his body like a sudden cold wind. The musket was useless, for no bullet could harm the horrible thing that lashed at the mare with a thorn branch. The moonlight saw a head like an ape, with horns, a skin of bristling hair, red glowing eyes and flashing teeth. It clutched at Caribou's mane with one hand, riding bareback.

11

Suddenly the thought came to the frightened Louis of an old way used to exorcise demons. Reaching up he seized the holy water font which hung at the head of all good *habitant's* beds. Then as the horse and rider passed beneath him, *Le Cavalier* threw both font and water crashing down on the head of the horned one.

A horrible shriek, the snorting of the terrified horse smote Louis' ears. Caribou reared, then in spite of the fiend's efforts, plunged into the half frozen lake.

Louis rushed down stairs and bolted for the beach, musket still in hand. But all that could be seen were widening ripples in the black water.

Le Cavalier fired his musket into the air as a signal for help. His neighbor, in nightshirt and cap, came running. Sadly Louis told the tale. The broken font, the thorn whip and the missing horse proved the truth of his story.

From that day to this, all of the *habitants* of Grosse Pointe, mark their horses with the cross.

And here the raconteur knocked the ashes from his pipe, bade his listeners good night and blew out the candle.

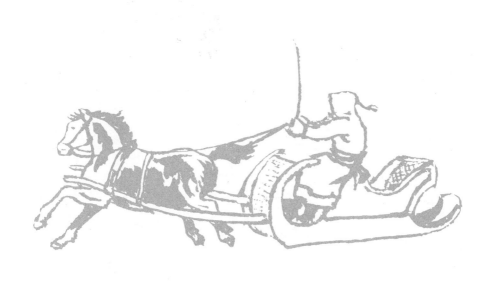

THE
RED
DWARF

4

Candles blazed through the tall windows of the banquet hall while inside at a table, set with costly silver and porcelain, sat a company of French officers. In spite of the gaiety and revelry, there was no doubt of the importance of the guests. They had gathered at the castle of St. Louis in Quebec to toast their guest of honor, Monsieur La Mothe Cadillac. He had just returned from France with a commission of Commandant, and a grant of a tract of land fifteen acres square on le Detroit, the Straits, where he would build a fort and locate a colony.

Cadillac had already achieved a distinguished career as a soldier and for five years was commandant at Fort de Buade at Michilimackinac. Whenever he had traveled through "the Straits," the Detroit river, he had been impressed with its location and possibilities. It could serve as a military post against their enemies, the Iroquois, and could help shut off the hated English from trade with the western tribes.

Now as the wine flowed from the excellent cellars of the castle, a servant whispered a message into The Governor of New France, Louis de Calliere's ear.

De Calliere announced to his guests that an old fortune teller wished an audience with them all. In high spirits and at the thought of some added entertainment, the entire company cried *"Oui, Monsieur!"*

The servant opened the door of the banquet hall and in came an old woman. She was very tall, dark complexioned, with glittering eyes and strange clothing.

"What is your name?" asked Cadillac.

In a deep, accented voice, she answered, "They call me *Mère Minique, La Sorcière.*" (Mother Minique, the sorcerer).

On her left shoulder perched a large but very thin black cat. As each officer held out his palm to be read, the cat would lick her ear. To some it meant the devil was giving her information.

There were expressions of surprise or laughter as she read the messages in the outstretched palms. At last she came to Cadillac.

Skeptical as always, the Commandant said. "*Ma bonne Mère,* tell me of the future, I care nothing for the past."

The Sorceress stared deeply into Cadillac's bold eyes. Then she took a basin from underneath her cape and into it poured a clear heavy liquid from a carved silver vial. She then held La Mothe Cadillac's hand, and gazed into the basin.

"Sieur", she said, "yours is a strange destiny. You will soon go on a dangerous journey, you will found a great city which will one day have more *habitants* than all of New France today. You will have many children." She paused. But Cadillac, thoroughly interested now, asked her to continue.

The Old Woman's face grew sad. "Sieur, I wish that you had not asked me to go on, for I see dark clouds rising. And your star shows but dimly. Your intent to sell brandy to the savages against the wishes of the Jesuit priests will cause you much trouble. In years to come there will be much blood shed. The Indians will be treacherous and the hated English will struggle for possession. But under their flag it will reach a greater degree of prosperity than you could dream. But you shall not see it, for France will claim your last sigh."

"Shall my children inherit my properties?" asked Cadillac, hopefully.

"Your future and the future of your family is in your hands. Beware of ambition and be careful not to offend *Nain Rouge,* the Red Dwarf. Should you do this, nothing will be left for your

16

children and your name will hardly be remembered in the city you will found."

There was silence around the table now. Gone were the jesting and the toasts. Clutching her pieces of silver, the Sorceress and her cat left the room. The party was over.

Cadillac, returning to his wife, jested at the prophecy. But his wife instead of being amused, seemed deeply troubled.

Early the next morning, La Mothe Cadillac said farewell to Quebec and set off by canoe for his new lands. With him were fifty soldiers of the *Compagnies Franches de la Marine,* fifty workmen and voyageurs, and a Rocollet and Jesuit priest.

Cadillac wished to take the shorter route by way of Lake Erie but because of Indian danger, the Governor insisted they take the older northern route. They left the 5th of June, reached Georgian Bay by way of the Ottawa River, then coasted down the Lake Huron's eastern shore. On the 20th, the canoes arrived at Old Fort St. Joseph now abandoned, and by the 24th, 1701, landed at Detroit.

On the next day pickets for a new fort were erected, a store house built and a salute was given by the guns they had brought. The Fort was named Fort Ponchartrain after the Count who had given Cadillac his commission.

Detroit was founded, and so far the fortune teller's predictions had been right. The settlement began to grow and the records of Ste. Anne's Church show that from 1704 to 1707 the annual birthrate was fourteen.

Then in May 1707 all of Cadillac's dreams seemed to be coming true. And faithful to the French tradition, a Maypole was erected in front of the Cadillac's fine home. The *habitants,* hat in hand, came to pay him homage. A youth climbed up the tall pole shouting *"Vive le Roi,* (long live the King) *Vive le Seigneur Cadillac du Detroit!"* There were cheers, the roll of drums, the sound of trumpets and the roar of cannon. Tables were spread under the shade tree and food and drink was given to all.

That evening just at dusk after the guests had left, Cadillac and his wife strolled in the King's Garden. He told her of his dreams and ambitions, how his children would inherit wealth and how his name would become illustrious. Just then two weary revellers passed speaking rather loudly.

"*Ah, oui,*" said one. "Our Seigneur and the *Dos Blanc,* meaning white backs, referring to the light grey coats of the soldiers, carry themselves very high, while we poor *habitants* pay double for everything!"

"Things cannot go on for long like this," said the other. "My wife a few nights ago saw *Nain Rouge* . . . . .".

Cadillac's wife grasped her husband's hand. "Did you hear? They spoke of seeing the terrible *Nain Rouge.*"

"What of that?" asked Cadillac.

"Beware of the Red Dwarf is what the Sorceress told you!"

"T'was but the prattling of an old crone," laughed le Seigneur.

Suddenly, across their path, came a dwarfed figure, red bearded, red haired, and clothed in a French coat of the old style. In his hand he carried a stout stick. His eyes were red coals, his teeth the fangs of a wolf.

"It is *Nain Rouge.*" whispered Cadillac's wife.

But before she could say more, Cadillac lifted his walking stick and struck the dwarf across his humped shoulders. "Get out of my way, you red imp!" he shouted.

A fiendish, mocking laugh answered him, and the monster was gone.

Cadillac's wife crossed herself with trembling hands. "*Mon Dieu,*" she cried, "we are finished!" And she burst into tears.

And so the prophecy of the Old Sorceress came true. Cadillac was later arrested in Montreal, forced to sell his rights in Detroit, and finally died in France. His children inherited nothing.

From that day forward people spoke of the demon who was last reported seen in 1805 when the city of Detroit burned to the ground.

THE DEVIL'S MILL

5

At the place called Presque Isle on Lake Erie's western shore, a great battle was fought between the French and their Indian allies, against the Fox tribe. When it was over the ground was covered with dead on both sides. The Fox were defeated and their bodies left for the crow and the gull. Called the Grave of the Fox Nation, the place lay deserted for many years because of the tragedy that had taken place there, and the spirits that were supposed to haunt the spot.

Years passed, when an *habitant* named Jean, and his older sister Josette, built a stone mill. Jean was a quiet, sombre man, far different from the fun-loving *Canadiens*. Rarely did he visit Detroit to the south, and on his visits never partook of the *cidre*, the sports or the singing nor did he speak to the smiling daughters of the habitants.

Both the habitants and the girls of the fort, asked the *coureurs des bois*, why Jean was so unfriendly. These woods rangers traveled everywhere and were able to furnish any gossip that might be asked for. The *coureurs* would only shrug their shoulders and say that *le pauvre Jean*, poor Jean, had been unfortunate in love as a youth and had vowed never to marry.

Josette through thrift and the sale of her delicious *croque-cignales*, a kind of doughnut, or her *gallette au beurre*, a butter and milk bread, saved enough to buy half of the mill. All went well and they lived peacefully beside the lake. Then one day

21

Josette fell sick. Jean did his clumsy best to help her but to little avail. As she began to fail, Jean began to make careful inquiries as to whom she would leave her half of the mill. Cross, from her suffering and his constant questions, Josette at last accused him of caring for her only to get her money. And in final desperation screamed out "I will leave it to the devil".

In three months she was dead. And that same night with the candles flickering beside the coffin, a great storm arose. The waves crashed against the shore, the winds shrieked their path around the point while tongues of lightening stabbed the ground and thunder rolled like artillery. In their homes, the *habitants* crossed themselves and told their beads. All at once a tremendous shock seemed to all but devour the island. The old stone mill split in half while a strong smell of sulphur filled the air. Then above the sound of the storm, came the sound of hideous laughter from the shattered stones. The devil had come for his share.

For years after, when a storm came out of the northeast followed by thunder and lightening, it was said that a hairy figure with a horned head and forked tail tipped with fire, eyes darting flame, could be seen at the mill trying to put together the ruined machinery to grind the devil's grist. The marshes were filled with dancing flames. These lights were called *feu-follet* or Will-o-the-wisps, by the *habitants*, trying to lure the unsuspecting stranger to help grind the devil's grist.

THE
WHITE
LADIES

6

The year was 1721. Outside Fort Michilimackinac the tribes had gathered for a council, Chippewa, Ottawa and some Potowatomi. Speaking to them was a tall Black Robe, a Jesuit Priest. When he finished there was a loud roar of discontent from the assembled warriors. For the Black Robe had just told them that no more brandy would be sold.

From the center of the grunting, murmuring crowd arose a chief. Known as a great orator he poured out his anger. "We know," he said, "that the white man's milk does us no good, it steals our tongues and our hands. But you have made us taste it and now we cannot do without it. If you refuse us, we shall get it from your enemies the English!" Drawing his blanket haughtily about him he strode off toward his village followed by his angry warriors.

The commandant was annoyed. It was not against his principles to give a gill of brandy for a pound of beaver skins, for, "every white man's hand weighed a pound . . ." which meant it was the traders custom to press their hands on the fur scale, adding to the weight. Calling aside a *coureur des bois* named Guillaume, he whispered that he would protect the traders if he should take a cask of brandy to the Indians and they would divide the furs.

Guillaume, the cask under one arm, set off.

When he arrived at the Indian village he found the older

chiefs in council but the young bloods were wandering about. To them he proposed a game of bowl. The stakes would be measures of brandy for furs. They eagerly accepted and ran to their round topped wigwams for pelts. Someone brought the Indian gambling game, a wooden bowl containing small carved pieces of bone which when tossed in the air fell into different winning combinations. Soon a huge pile of glossy beaver pelts were there beside Guillaume, and his eyes glistened as he thought of the profit they would bring.

Soon the sounds of the gamblers drew even the chiefs into the game, for gambling was an important part of Indian life.

The trader's winnings increased and the Indians drank the brandy as fast as they could win a gill. By nightfall, the players lay strewn about the campground, sleeping off the brandy fumes while Guillaume, strapped the heavy bundle of pelts on his back and started back to the Fort. He too had drunk his share, so he ambled slowly through the woods enjoying the cool night and the heavy load on his back.

Suddenly, he was startled to see small white shapes flitting about an oak tree. Moving fearfully closer he realized that they were "*Les Dames Blanches*" or white ladies, tiny fairies believed in by all the *habitants*. As soon as they saw Guillaume, they caught hold of him and with peals of laughter made him dance until he was ready to drop. In vain he pleaded for them to stop but they only laughed the louder. His pack fell off and the fairies quickly seized a pelt for each. As he saw his valuable beaver skins disappearing, Guillaume chased the white ladies, shouting for them to stop. Round and round they went until he grew dizzy. Each time he thought he had caught one of them, they would disappear into the ground leaving a tiny spring of clear water. Finally he gave up. Gathering the few pelts left, he staggered onward toward the fort.

Now on the route, lay an Indian burying ground. On several of the burial mounds was a cage with a live bird. This was the custom, that when an Indian maiden died, a young bird was caged about her grave. Then when it began to sing, the bird was tenderly released and would carry the girl's spirit to the Happy Hunting Ground.

Now their doleful sounds only deepened Guillaume's depression and he began to run. Suddenly a wild shriek rent the quiet night and looking up he saw a *Loup Garou* or Were Wolf. These were ferocious creatures that could change from man to wolf at will. Before the *coureur des bois* could move, the fiend had leaped straight onto his back and both rolled in a heap down the sand hill. Somehow, the trader wrenched free and fled to the fort where he breathlessly told the tale. Next morning he and some unbelieving friends went to the spot of the night's terrors. To their amazement, the grass around the oak tree was singed and everywhere little springs of water were bubbling. Where the *Loup Garou* had disappeared, a sulphur spring now gurgled.

Convinced of Guillaume's story, they returned to the Fort to tell the others. And thus the tale survives to this day.

ANGELIQUE AND THE WOLF-MAN

7

O n a small farm near Detroit, lived a beautiful young girl, Angelique, and her father Honoré. Their mother, poor soul, had died when the child was born and the grief stricken father had left Montreal to take up a new life in the *pays sauvage*. Honoré loved his daughter deeply. For her he chose the softest bear skin for her bed, fawn skin for her Indian style dresses. He even had French clothes brought from Montreal for Church going and celebrations.

When she grew up he taught her many things, to skin the beaver and muskrat and deer which he brought home. She learned also to stretch them on the drying frame. In the fort and among the habitants, all agreed that Angelique excelled all in cooking the *poisson blanc* or whitefish, *poisson dore* or pike, or prepare *cochon au lait,* suckling pig, to just the right shade of golden, crackling brown.

She was a happy girl, constantly singing bright French songs while spinning. In the long winter evenings, her fingers were never idle, plaiting straw into hats which she sold, knitting socks, drying corn. All of these items brought her enough to buy pretty ribbons for her hair or a length of calico for a new dress.

Her beauty was such, that at corn huskings and dances, she was the queen, fascinating the local boys with her dark eyes and shining black hair. None could compare when it came to dancing the *gigue à deux* or the graceful *danse ronde*.

It was young Phillipe who finally won her heart. Honoré gave his consent and in the evenings Phillipe would take his fianceé for quiet canoe rides in the moonlight. Happily they would talk of the wedding to come and of the new home that her husband was building for them.

All the world seemed full of wildflowers and sunshine that spring as the wedding day drew near. Then, one afternoon as Angelique was gathering wildflowers for the table, a strange figure flitted past her among the trees. At first she paid no mind, thinking it one of the local lads playing tricks. Then in a clearing, Angelique stopped dead still, her hands clasped her saint's medal, heart pounding. Standing there in her path was a *Loup Garou*. He had robbed some *habitant* of a coat and hat, and had tucked his wolf's tail away. In his hand he held a cane like some Parisienne dandy. When Angelique did not move, he gave her a lovesick leer, showing his sharp wolf's teeth and lolling tongue beneath a bristly muzzle. Then he started toward her, arms outstretched.

Dropping her flowers the girl fled and reached her cabin just in time to slam and bolt the door.

When word reached the neighbors they set out to find and kill the beast. All attempts were fruitless however, he seemed to lead a charmed existence. One hunter nearly succeeded. From a silver coin he molded a bullet. Waiting beside the path he spied the wolf-man and fired. But instead of killing the monster it only cut off his tail. The tail was dried and stuffed and thought by the Indians to be a powerful fetish.

The wedding day came at last and all nature seemed to be waiting for the fair Angelique and the handsome Phillipe. At last the two entered the Fort church followed by all the *habitants* in their best clothing. In front of the altar, decorated with flowers, they knelt and were wed. While the bell rang happily from its wooden belfry, the two went to the sacristy and wrote their names in the registry, then hurried off to their new home. There they waited on the grass to greet their friends. Refreshments were served, the fiddles sounded and in true French Canadian fashion, they prepared to celebrate for several days.

30

Suddenly while the merry making was at its height, the terrible *Loup Garou* dashed into the crowd, seized the beautiful Angelique, and carried her into the forest. The crowd was stunned, but Phillipe started off in instant pursuit hearing the screams of his lovely bride. The others followed, while women and children and the curé said prayers.

Late that night the men returned without Phillipe. They had been unable to find the wolf-man and the bridegroom too seemed to have disappeared. The next morning they went out at dawn and found him wandering around and around in the swamp, clutching a bit of Angelique's wedding dress in his trembling hand. When they tried to question him, he only stared at them with eyes rimmed with madness. They led him home, but daily he returned to the swamp to stare into the slimy waters.

A year passed while Phillipe grew gaunt with sorrow. At the marriage of his sister, however he seemed to improve and after the ceremony, suddenly rushed into the woods. He did not return until sunset, his clothing torn, his eyes wild as if he had been chasing the *Loup Garou*. It was then they heard the story. He had indeed tracked the fiend to the waters edge. And here, the animal seeing no escape from the stone on which he stood, stretched out his arms as if beckoning the evil one. At that moment a giant catfish rose to the surface, opened his mouth and the *Loup Garou* vanished.

The footprint of the demon may still be seen on the rock, and to this day no *habitant* will eat catfish.

SKY
HUNT

8

There once lived along the eastern shore of Lake Michigan, a hunter, Michel *dit le chasseur,* or the hunter. Above all things he liked the chase, and his friends could never get him to join in any other sports. It was said he was born with a gun in his hand, hence his nickname. He would disappear for weeks and then return laden with game.

After one of these trips, Michel was more silent than usual. Even among his friends he was reluctant to tell of his adventures or the excellence of his favorite musket.

It wasn't until later that the mystery was solved. One day during the hunt, while chasing a deer, Michel had discovered a new cabin deep in the forest. At the door stood a beautiful young girl carefully dressing a wound in the side of a young buck. Michel saw that it was the deer he had wounded. He learned that the girl's name was Marianne, and that she had come into the spring woods to help her father collect maple sap to make syrup.

As sometimes happens, the two fell in love, he with her gentle beauty, she with his strength and honesty. It was decided that they would wed at the church at Michilimackinac in September.

One day while strolling along the beach discussing plans for the wedding on the morrow, Marianne admitted that she suffered from *serrement de coeur,* or squeezing and pressing of her heart, and feared that their happiness might not last. But Michel only laughed at such an idea. He was strong enough for both, he said.

But to himself he wondered. Once married, would he have to give up his life in the woods and become a stay at home married man? He left his fiancée and returned shortly with several hunters, guns in hand, followed by their dog, *Tache* or "spots." While they were untying the bateau from its moorings, Michel pointed out to Marianne, a flock of ducks flying toward the flats. This, he said, would be his farewell hunt.

Marianne hid her face in her hands, her slender body shaking with sobs.

"Ah, Michel," she begged. "Do not leave me, for I fear you shall never return!"

Michel tried to comfort her, but she told him how she had heard a screech owl in the tree near her window, and at the same time there was a barking of dogs and a ringing of bells in the night. They were sure signs of misfortune.

Michel looked into her sorrowful face, torn between his love for her and the companionship of his friends. At last, hearing the calls of his companions he kissed her tenderly.

"Fear not, *ma petite*," he said gently. "I shall return tomorrow at dawn, dead or alive," he added in jest.

Soon the hunters were paddling off, *Tache*, the dog barking his farewell, Michel waving his red sash.

At dawn, Marianne awoke and hurried to the sandy beach. It was a perfect day with the lake bluer than ever before and the dark forests beckoning with their splashes of red maple and yellow birch leaves. Today was her wedding day. Why did Michel tarry? Hour after hour she waited, praying to Ste. Anne, the patron saint of mariners, to guide her lover home.

In the afternoon, others whose husbands or brothers had gone with Michel, came to join her vigil. But as night fell, there was still no sign of the hunters.

Day after day, Marianne watched and waited, scanning the great lake and empty sky. Snow fell, and melted again. Still no sign of her husband to be. Somehow she seemed hopeful as if held up by faith alone.

34

And then one evening she looked up and saw Michel's boat in the clouds. In a voice still strong but far away he called to her. "I will come for you in a year and a day." This was followed by the barking of his dog.

A year and a day passed. Now Marianne grew more pale, thinner. On the promised day Marianne had herself dressed in her bridal gown and carried to the beach. It was much like the day Michel had left, with ducks flying toward the marsh.

Suddenly the dying girl pointed at the sky. "See!" she cried out, "there is Michel in the bateau with his dog. Listen to *Tache* barking. Here they come and they are beckoning to me. Michel, Michel I am coming . . ."

And with that, her faithful spirit leaped upward to join her spirit bridegroom.

Her friends stared with awe to where she had gone and saw a boat drifting in the billowing clouds and heard the echo of a barking dog grow faint and fade into silence.

This vision has been reported in different form over many years by habitants of French Canada. Sometimes a canoe is manned by twelve men with a barking dog at its bow. At other times a shaggy black dog is seen running on the water, tracking game. Once in seven years a solitary horseman, musket in hand, rides the skies, followed by a pack of hounds.

But he who sees the vision, is sure of one thing. Death awaits them or their dear ones.

LES
FEU
FOLLET

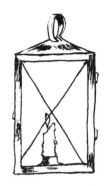

9

Marie and her husband Robert along with their baby, Jean, lived in their home outside of Fort Michilimackinac. One warm summer day, Marie's cousin, young Jacques from Montreal, came to pay a visit. Marie was delighted and when Robert suggested that he take a day's trip to meet with some *coureurs de bois* near the Ottawa Indian village of *L'Arbre Croche,* the Crooked Tree, Marie was quite content to stay at home with her young cousin, the baby and a Pani woman servant. Panis were Indian slaves, prisoners taken in Indian wars who served as domestics.

All went well until evening when storm clouds began to form over the lake and white caps showed their plumes far out in the lead colored water.

The women watched it approach the cabin. Now the sky was very dark except for the brilliant lightning forking lakeward. Marie began to worry about Robert and asked the Pani woman to split some slivers off the Christmas Log (always preserved year by year) and to throw them on the fire to prevent the thunder from falling. She then glanced at the door and was relieved to see a branch of white thorn still in place. This bush was thought to be a divine lightening rod. The custom had probably come from the fact that thorns such as these had crowned the Saviour's head.

Gradually the rumble of thunder and the lightening

passed. By now it was dark. Marie's fears began to rise once more as her husband failed to return. Going to the window she peered into the darkness. Suddenly all were startled by a shrill whistle. Even Jean in his crib, began to cry. Quickly, Marie slammed the shutters clossed, and bolted them. "I saw the *feu follet* dancing over the fields, if I had not shut it out it would have entered and strangled us!" she cried. *"Le Bon Dieu* preserve Robert this night!"

Her cousin tried to comfort her. "Do not fear, Robert your husband can take care of himself." he said. "If you like, now that the rain has stopped, we can go looking for him." A sturdy young man, he moved toward the door confidently trying to ease his cousin's fears. Jean was sound asleep and the Pani woman was a good nursemaid. Marie made up her mind. Robert was never late, something must have happened on the trail.

"Let us go," she said, wrapped a shawl around her shoulders and handed a lantern to Jacques. "I know the path well."

As they walked Jacques, trying to keep her mind from her missing husband asked, "What are the *feu follet* like at Michilimackinac, cousin?"

"They are not always dangerous and they appear as lights above swampland. When twin lights are seen in the twilight, they are called Castor and Pollus and this is a happy omen."

"This I had not heard," said Jacques, lantern held high, watching the dim trail ahead.

"But," Marie continued, "When a single light appears it is named Helène. Then he who sees it must throw himself on the ground and cover his face. For the light holds an evil magic that lures the traveler to desert bogs or steep ravines then leaves him there to die . . . But Robert does not believe in them" Jacques shook his head. *"Grand-père* who came from Caen in Normandy said that the *feu follet* there, are male and female and are supposed to be those who have sinned against purity. Therefore the Normans call maidens who have sinned, *fourolle,* such as *'fourolle* Jeanne' or *'fourelle* Mignonette'. The Evil One gives them power to turn themselves into bright lights leading travelers to their deaths."

38

Marie shuddered.

"Perhaps it is time we shouted for Robert" said Jacques. Together they called out his name again and again, for now the ground was getting miry and frogs croaked dismally close by. The lantern threw weird shapes against the dark trees, and Marie held her shawl tighter around her shoulders. Still there was no answer. Desperate, the young wife uttered one last despairing cry. It was answered instantly by a pistol shot. With a shout they both sprang forward through the underbrush. There in the swamp was a figure up to his waist in the sucking mud. It was Robert.

Together they made a bridge with their hands and soon the weary traveler was in his wife's tearful embrace.

As they made their way happily homeward, he told his story. Returning later than expected from the village, he had become lost in the storm. All at once he had seen a light and followed it only to plunge into the swamp. He cried out for help until he grew hoarse and all he heard was the mocking laughter of goblins. At last, when he thought all hope gone, he had heard his wife's final cry. It was then he had fired his pistol.

"Perhaps now, *mon chéri,* you will believe in *les feu follet*?" asked Marie.

Robert nodded, thoughtfully, "You were right, *ma petite.* I believe!"

SAN
SOUCI

10

When the *habitants* gathered to join in celebration with the returning voyageurs, one of the favorite tales was that of *San Souci,* an ancient mare whose name meant "Without Care." It seems this horse belonged to an old bachelor at Fort Detroit, Jean Beaugrand, and had lived far longer than the memory of any *habitant.* His escapades were always the course of much laughter over a jug of *cidre* and wondrous tales they were. Jean, the owner, was also the subject of much laughter among the children of the fort because he was forever mumbling to himself.

Jean Beaugrand worked for the Indian agent Robert, who owned a fine French house where traders, visiting dignitaries and Indian chiefs, often gathered to sup and drink in front of the huge fireplace.

It was a wonder to all how old *San Souci* had managed to survive for so long. For it was her want to visit the cornfields or gardens of the neighbors once a week, escaping under a hail of sticks and stones. But no matter how much she ate, she grew thinner until she looked like an ancient white scarecrow. No fence could be built to keep her out and a story was told that she even jumped the 12 foot palisades on occasion. She had been shot at, whipped, clubbed, but her only reaction was a laying back of ears and a flurry of hooves. On warm sunny days she wandered down the narrow streets until she found a dog fight to observe or a group of loafers talking politics. There she stood, head hanging, apparently enjoying the conversation. If a joke was told, she would open her mouth and neigh in laughter. At other times she merely shook her head like some ancient sage. But of her own thoughts, no one knew except her master, Jean. When he appeared her ears would prick up and she would follow him behind the barn, forgetting her usual ambling pace, but nearly trotting in hope of food to come.

One night a number of French, and Indians, were seated around the agent's fire. The cider had run out and the chiefs were clamoring for brandy. One of the chiefs asked permission to visit the cellar for a bottle.

"You will have to waken Old Beaugrand," said the agent. "He has the key." The chief whose name was Muck-wah Mok-i-mon or Bear Knife, left for the key but returned in evident terror. He told the agent, Robert, whose Indian name was "Obitose," meaning "Yellow-hair," that he had peeked into Jean's room only to see Beaugrand and San Souci both seated at a table, chatting together. This was not strange for an Indian to believe as they all looked on animals as being able to speak under certain magical conditions. But the agent, to the horror of the Chief, rose from his chair in anger.

"We shall see about this," he said, sternly. Followed by several of the guests he climbed the ladder to Jean's room determined to find out the truth of the matter. One Frenchman put his eye to a crack and swore later that he saw Old Jean playing at whist with the horse. Both were drinking from pewter cups and seemed to be enjoying themselves.

As the agent kicked open the door to end this foolishness he saw the old mare leap through the open window. Whereupon, Jean, accused now of working with the Devil, insisted that he was only drinking a little cider and that the mare was in her stable below.

Muck-wah Mok-i-mon would not believe but what Jean had been talking with the mare. Ever after he considered Yellow Hair as "big medicine" and from that day on the agent, Obitose, had great influence over the Indians for so bravely driving off an evil spirit.

THE FRENCH CAPTAIN

11

In 1760 when the lilies of France were replaced by the British red ensign, many *habitants* remained in the Great Lakes area, especially in Fort Detroit. Fort Michilimackinac too had its share. However by 1780, most of the fort and town had been removed across the straits to Mackinac Island and rebuilt. But the old tales remained and some new legends were created. One dealt with Jean Cecire.

In 1805, the militia was revived at Fort Detroit. The first regiment was made up of eight companies. To the Americans now in control of what had once been French and then British lands, the desire to remain friendly with the French seemed an important diplomatic act. Therefore they commissioned Jean Cecire, Captain in the First Regiment of Michigan. He was pleased beyond belief and became so impressed with the importance of his new commission, that every detail of his dress and bearing were designed to impress on all his gloried rank.

Of course the *habitants* had many a chuckle at his expense. With a typical shrug of the shoulders they enjoyed his conceit with all the good humor of the French Canadian.

Jean's favorite occupation was to watch the regular troops drill. Their severe discipline and military exactness puzzled him somewhat and he decided it must be due to the words of command being given in English in which there was hidden magic. His knowledge of English was as slight as his writing ability. In fact to cover up the latter, he used the muster role and after calling out the names of his men, would place a pin prick after their names when absent. But as fluid as his French, English stuck in his throat except for some words which by sheer will power he learned.

At last the time of training arrived. Captain Jean was ordered to drill his company on the parade field. No great general ever surveyed his armies with greater pride. And while some of his men were in parts of uniform, others wore the colorful dress of the *voyageurs* and *habitants,* colored sashes, *tuques* (caps) moccasins, leggings, and hunting shirts, the motley crew filled the Captain's gallic heart with pride.

Puffing out his chest, Captain Jean ordered his sergeant to call the role while the Captain stood by in full regimentals.

Sergeant: "Attention *Compagnie des Canadiens-Français.* Answer your name when I call, if you please. Tock Tock Livernois?"

No answer. At last a voice says,: Not here, gone catch hees horse in bush . . . "

Capt. "Sergeant, put peen hole in dat man! *Allons!*"

Sergeant: Laurent Bondy?"

"Here, Sah!"

Claude Campau?"

"Here, Monsieur."

"Antoine Saliotte?"

Someone answers. Little *bèbe* came last night at his house, must stay home."

Captain. "Sergeant. Put pen preek after dat name."

After the roll was called the Captain prepared to drill his company.

"*Marchee! Mes camarades, deux par deux* (two and two) like oxen and when you come to dat stump, stop!"

They straggled to the place, looking in their colorful garb like a drunken rainbow. Disgusted, the Captain gave them a short break. But instead of resting, *au militaire,* they rushed off, one to smoke, another to polish his old carbine, while others sat on the grass spinning yarns.

The Captain tried again. This time his shouted command was, "*Marchee* as far as dat old shoe in de road, den turn." Right, *gauche*, left, shoulder muskeet!" Advance, back!" Drill Fineesh!"

In all fairness, Captain Jean led his men with great courage in the field but in the Battle of Mongaugon, he lost his Sergeant and his men began to waver. Brave Jean, try as he would, could not think of the words of command he so badly needed to rally them. At last he broke forth:

"Fix yourself as the brave Sergeant did, den by Gar, follow me!"

Many years later, the Captain's son, a Lieutenant of Militia met old Chief Oshkosh at an inn. Quietly smoking his pipe the wrinkled chief looked up to see this uniformed Lieutenant swagger in. Many there knew how Oshkosh felt about militia and decided to have some fun so they introduced Cecire to the chief. The Indian put down his pipe and gazed at the soldier.

"Infantry?" he asked
"No" was the reply
"Dragoon?"
"No"
"Artillery?"
"No"

Oshkosh, the famous lieutenant of Chief Black Hawk, paused. Then suddenly a light dawned.

He leaped to his feet and hissed in disgust, "Milish?"
"Yes" was the brave reply.
"Oh, hell!" said Oshkosh and bolted for the door.

TWO
FISHERMEN

12

Sault Ste. Marie, north of Fort Michilimackinac, place of the fierce rapids, was long known to the Redman as the home of the whitefish. It was here that two unmarried brothers lived. One was Augustin, the elder, and the younger, Henri. Their skill in fishing and in the making and mending nets was well known. Also well known, was Augustin's belief in the supernatural, and Henri's use of profane language. Augustin had often told Henri that should he meet a goblin, there were two things that could save him. The first was to place two sticks in the form of a cross. The second, and more powerful, was to ask *le lutin*, "What day of the month is Christmas?" Goblins were never very well up on the calendar and would reply by asking the same question. Woe to the person who did not know the answer or hesitated in answering.

But Henri always answered by calling a goblin nothing but a *bête puante* or stinking beast.

All went well for the brothers. They were known as outstanding fishermen and traded their daily catch for their neighbor's corn or *L'huile d'ours*, bear's fat, a pleasant addition to their menu. However, like all fishermen, they were dependent on the weather. Often a sudden frost in autumn would freeze their nets in the ice. While a sudden spring thaw might break up the nets and carry them away. Each time they were able to start over but when luck deserted them, the seines would be

49

empty except for a few herring instead of the wonderful white-fish or an occasional muskelunge. Finally after one particularly bad season, Augustin said, "Let us consult *le bon père*."

"*Sacré bleu*," he grumbled. "What good will that do?"

Henri who had been rebuked several times for profanity by the priest himself, was not friendly.

"He can do something," insisted Augustin. "Some enemy has *donné le sort*, bewitched, our fishery. If you will consult le curé, I will go,"

The brothers separated, Henri to look for new fishing grounds, Augustin to consult the priest. Augustin after explaining the problem to the curé listened hopefully.

"Ah, mon fils, my son, choose St. Patrick as your partner. And as you know it is the custom to bring the first game and first catch of the season to the church door where it is auctioned off. From this, the poor benefit. Share your fish with the Saint, and sell his portion for the poor."

Augustin agreed and made a solemn vow to share. That evening he cast his nets, promising it would be the Saint's portion, the morning haul would be his own. When the nets of evening came in they were brimming with fish, but in the morning they were empty. Strongly tempted to keep St. Patrick's share, Augustin nontheless remembered his vow and in spite of the jeers of Henri, sold the fish and gave the money to the poor. However the bad luck on the morning's catch continued. In desperation he again consulted *le curé*.

"Your simple faith and honesty touch me, Augustin," said *le curé*. They will bring you rewards. Hereafter divide only the proceeds from each net with the Saint. Your honesty is above reproach. Few would have done as you."

From that day forward, Augustin became so successful that he became known as the lucky fisherman of the Sault.

As for Henri, he was not doing too well, yet refused to share as his brother was doing. Furthermore, he kept making threats. "You will be lured into the lake and turned into a whitefish," he threatened. Or, "Do you remember the legend of *Les Saulteurs*, Indians of the Sault, how *le poisson blanc*, or whitefish, were formed? How the brains of a woman were dashed out to

50

make the fish? Your partner, the Saint, will play you a trick. Did he not eat pork on Friday by dipping it into holy water and changing it into trout? Beware."

But Augustin only smiled. Then one day, he was startled when Henri came dashing into the house in a terrible state.

"Something awful will happen to us," he wailed. "*Mon dieu!* As I was leaving my boat five miles from here, the cock crew which as you know, meant I would meet someone on the road. As I was trotting along in my two-wheeled cart, I saw a lady's fur muff by the road. It seemed strange to see such a thing in summer and I got down to pick it up. As soon as I reached for it, however, it began rolling. I became angry and ran after it but it kept evading me. Suddenly I became frightened. This was no muff but some goblin wishing to do me harm. I leaped into my cart and trotted off as fast as I could but now the terrible thing began chasing me!"

"It was the *Manchon Roulant*, the rolling muff," said Augustin crossing himself." If you had carried holy water instead of brandy in that flask of yours, you would have been safe. Now you must go back and ask it what day Christmas comes on."

Trembling with fear, Henri returned and sure enough the terrible thing was waiting. Crossing himself, he carefully approached the rolling fur, and suddenly seized it! But instead of asking the Christmas question, he blurted out terrible oaths. Instantly there streamed forth a blast as though from a furnace, and a awful odor struck him full in the face. In terror, Henri dropped the fearful thing and dashed for the lake and plunged in.

Ever after when Augustin reminded him that it was his punishment for swearing, or when the name *Manchon Roulant* was mentioned, Henri quickly ran from the room.

GODFROI LE GÉANT

13

In the small village of Michilimackinac lived a poor widow with a son named *Godfroi dit Le Géant,* or Godfrey called the Giant. While many, particularly the voyageurs, were small men, well able to fit into a canoe, Le Géant was nearly 7 feet tall with great powerful arms and hands. Although strong, he was quiet and gentle. He liked small animals and often treated injured birds until they were well. While the village liked him and treated him well, strangers drew back in horror at the sight of him. For it was said, that an old squaw had thrown a spell on his mother several months before he was born. She was a maker of baskets and a drinker of brandy. When under the influence of liquor, she would roam the streets, screaming like some wild beast. One night when her money was gone, she had beaten on the door of the poor widow. She, poor woman, was afraid to open it and thus the squaw pronounced her devilish curse. As a result, the boy's face was a mask of ugliness except for the clear blue eyes that looked emptily from their sockets. His face and body were covered with hair, his mouth was a mere hole which showed a pair of yellow fangs. And his speech was affected also, so that except for a few words, he made his needs known by signs.

Still, all at the fort respected his strength and his kindness to his poor mother, widowed years before by her husband who had drowned off Bois Blanc Island.

To support themselves, *Le Géant* fished from his wooden bateau and was skilled with the sail or paddle. In season he also gathered berries and nuts from the woods to sell.

He was fourteen before the curé allowed him to make his first communion. And while his intelligence had not been improved, he could make his way, helping gather firewood, doing heavy work and in general being a real part of the village.

When he was not working, he loved to sail his bateau out into the Straits often to Mackinac Island, or to St. Ignace on the mainland. This course was a dangerous one even for the Indians, but *Le Géant* seemed to travel it without mishap. Then one day something happened that was to change his life. He met a young woman, as frail and thin as he was strong. Her name was Thérèse and she had spent 12 years as a captive of the dreaded Iroquois. When recaptured, the good soldiers of Les Compagnies Franches de la Marine, the only French troops in the *pays sauvage*, wept to see her being treated as a slave. She was brought back to the Straits and now lived with an uncle who treated her no better.

When *Le Géant* saw her struggling to carry water on a neck yolk from the spring to her miserable cabin, he hurried to help and was amazed to see her gaze at him without fear but with gratitude.

For the first time he dared raise his eyes to meet a woman's and *Le Géant* fell in love.

Frail, raggedly dressed, barefooted without the shoes or stockings she had never owned, Thérèse looked like *un ange,* an angel, to Godfroi.

The first thing he did upon his return to the fort, was to buy her a pair of store shoes and a flowered dress which had come all the way from Montreal.

Hurrying to her uncle's cabin, he waited until she came to the spring and then managed to say, "Dress, Mam'selle? Shoes, Mam'selle? You take, eh?"

For the first time, Thérèse felt as though she was not an object of pity and a touch of color in her pale cheeks told of her happiness.

From that moment forward, the two loved each other.

Neither at 18 could think of why they should not always be together.

That night Godfroi told his mother of Thérèse and his love.

She found it quite right that her good son had found a *bonne amie,* or dear friend, and that he thought of marriage.

As is always true in a small community, it wasn't long before all knew the story of *Le Géant.* For on the following Sunday, he set out in his boat to ask Thérèse to go with him to high mass at the Church of Ste. Anne at Michilimackinac. Thérèse agreed.

Happily she brought out her new clothes, the flowered dress and the store shoes. All she lacked was a hat with feathers but a bright blue ribbon had to serve. As to her uncle, he was glad to have her married off and in his way he liked *Le Géant.*

On the tolling of the third bell for the high mass, *Le Géant* and Thérèse appeared at the church door, arm in arm.

No one wished to mock him, but many a smile was hidden behind a hand at the strange pair. The lovers entered the church and took a wooden pew near the carved altar. And there they heard the mass with great piety.

As they left, there were murmurs of *"Godfroi dit Le Géant* has a sweetheart. The Giant one wishes to be married!" were whispered among the crowd.

"He is a brave boy," said one. "But what hope for marriage with a monster face like his?" And that seemed to be the general feeling.

The doctor of the fort dined each Sunday with the cure. Over their brandy they decided that somehow the marriage must be stopped. For *Le Géant* to father children as ugly as himself, perhaps with the frail body and weak lungs of Thérèse, could not help but result in deformed children. Nothing was done then. There would be time when the marriage banns were to be placed.

Both were ignorant of the talk in the village. They went about their tasks as usual but each evening at dusk the lovers met on the beach. As poor as he was he always managed a cotton kerchief, a bit of ribbon, a fruit or bonbon, or a bouquet of wildflowers for his intended. Each time he offered them the same.

"*Bojou Mam'selle Thérèse.*"
"*Bojour, Godfroi.*"

And this was their conversation. They seated themselves on the side of the bateau which *Le Géant* had drawn up on the beach. There they sat, hand in hand, watching the sun set above the Straits.

At last there would be a call from the house. "Thérèse, oh Thérèse." It was the uncle.

"*Bonsoir, Thérèse!*"
"*Bonsoir, Godfroi!*"

Le Géant paddled or sailed back to the fort, Thérèse walked happily to the cabin.

And then, one month later, *Le Géant* seemed more joyful than ever. His blue eyes almost seemed to sparkle.

"*Bonjour, Thérèse!*"
"*Bonjour, Godfroi!*"

With hands that trembled, *Le Géant* took a small buckskin sack from his sash and withdrew a golden ring which he placed on the hand of the girl.

"Us to marry, Ste. Annes!"
"Oh, yes, Godfroi!"

And the young couple exchanged a kiss. It was their first.

The marriage they decided would be for Michaelmas so all that remained was to place the banns at the church. The uncle and widow had consented so that they need not see the notary for a marriage contract. There was no question of dowry or heritage. Both were too poor.

The next afternoon, *Le Géant* put on his best clothes and made his way to the house of the curé. He found him in the garden reciting his breviary.

"Bonjour, Godfroi." said he.
"*Bonjour M'sieu Curé.*" answered *Le Géant*.
"I hear, Godfroi that you have intention to marry."
"*Oui, M'sieu Curé.*"
"With Mademoiselle Thérèse?"

56

"*Oui, M'sieu Curé.*"

"It must not be thought of, *mon fils*, my son. You have no way to keep a wife and your poor mother, what of her with no one to give her bread."

Poor Godfroi looked as though he had been struck in the face. He almost staggered backward. Never had he thought of any difficulty in marrying. Hadn't his mother and the uncle agreed? What was the curé saying? His blue eyes grew blank with puzzlement.

Seeing the stricken giant, the cure said kindly, "Godfroi it must not be. You must wait until you are of age and have more means."

Again, *Le Géant* could not answer. A sob, twisted his mis-shapen face. All he knew was they could not marry. Perhaps never. Without thinking of arguing, he turned and ran for his boat. He could not bear to have the villagers see him weeping and the tears were beginning to come. Clasped at last in his mother's arms, he could only sob, "Me no marry Thérèse. Me die, maman . . ."

At last his mother spoke. "I will go to see the curé, my son. I see no reason why you two cannot be one." Throwing a shawl across her head, she started toward the beached bateau. Dumbly, *Le Géant* followed. And dumbly he waited as his mother trudged toward the house of the curé. He dared not hope and yet . . .

Back she came. *Le Géant* took one look at her sad face, then turned his own to the darkening sky, and howled like a wounded dog.

Back at their cabin, he could not eat. Thunder rolled outside and the sky grew dark as his thoughts. At last he ran from the cabin and in spite of his mother's pleas that a northeastern was coming, sprang into his boat, hoisted sail and was off into the rising seas.

Thérèse was waiting at her usual place. As she saw him approaching she ran toward the waves, arms outstretched. Only then did she see his stricken face.

"Godfroi, *mon cher*, what is it?" she begged.

Savagely he beached the boat, then seized her in his arms,

stammering broken phrases, wracked with sobs.

"*M'sieu le Curé,* no marry . . . too poor . . . too ugly me . . . me want to die!"

They stood together in the rain that was now driving across the water, bending the pines and poplars along the shore. Time seemed to cease as they stood, locked in each others arms, while the mounting waves tore at their feet.

It was nearly dawn when Thérèse finally drew away. For some reason perhaps presentiment, she said brokenly "*Adieu, mon cher!*"

"*Adieu, ma belle Thérèse!*" Goodbye, my beautiful Thérèse.

Shivering with cold she watched *Le Géant's* powerful arms shove the tiny craft into the white capped sea. Up went the sail, and with a final wave, he was gone.

Three days later they found the boat swamped near the shores of Mackinac Island. And although they fired the cannon at Fort Michilimackinac, hoping to bring up his body, Godfroi, *dit Le Géant,* was never seen again. As for Thérèse, a month later at Michaelmas, her body was carried to the cemetary of Ste. Anne's. Even in death, they were to be separated.

THE MAGIC TREE

14

The French voyageurs acquired some of their tales from the Indians of the Great Lakes. The Hurons were the first lake Indians to greet the French, and the Huron nation more readily accepted Christianity as preached by the Recollect and Jesuit priests than any other group. But old traditions die hard. The American Indian deeply religious, found it hard to accept the European God, and sometimes mixed both the old faith with the new. The following tale deals with Christianity as practiced by the early 17th Century missionaries and their Huron allies at Huronia, along the shore of Georgian Bay. Here the French built a stockaded village complete with barns, churches for the French and for the Indians, blacksmith shop, and other buildings. Today it has been reconstructed in all its excitement near Midland, Ontario. It is called Ste. Marie-Among-the-Hurons.

The story is told that having lost his only son, old Hurukay, a Huron, carved a likeness of his son in basswood, which he kept in his medicine bundle. Often he would take it out to help him forget that he was the last of his line and that none would live on to succeed him. Hurukay was a Christian, but often went to a sacred spot of the Indians called the Magic Tree. Here he would take out the wooden image of his only son and dream of happier days.

On Christmas Eve Hurukay made his way to the tree and

while sitting there in silence, had a dream. In the dream he saw a beautiful woman, a white woman, garbed in white standing before him. She reached down, smiling and touched the image he held in his hand. Hurukay awoke and upon seeing her said, "Why do you appear to me, I am only an old man, an Indian. You are a white woman and so young, like the granddaughter I might have had."

"Because I love, you, Hurukay as do your people. In your kindness and wisdom you have become a saint. The Gates of Heaven will open for you before the northern star dips to the edge of the sky."

"I know you now, cried Hurukay. "You are *Notre-Dame de Les Hurés,* Our Lady of the Huron."

"When I die," he continued, "I hope to rest my head at your feet in heaven."

Whereupon, the blessed Virgin took the carved image from his arms and lifted it to her breast where it awakened. It took the shape of the Infant Jesus with a halo glowing about his head. Both mother and child smiled at him, while he sat motionless at their feet.

No sooner had the vision vanished, than finding the statue once more in his lap, he ran to the village in a trance and arrived at the chapel as the bell tolled for midnight mass.

From his pew he watched the Huron chiefs and the Jesuit missionary kneel at the manger to sing a Christmas Carol. Written for the Indians by one of the missionaries, it told the story, in French, of the infant Jesus and his birth where he was wrapped in a robe made of rabbit skins as was the Huron custom. When they finished, Hurukay placed the image blessed by the Virgin in the empty manger, saying. "I found him under the Tree of Dreams. Then Hurukay sang his death song and while he knelt, breathed his last.

After his death, other Indians sought the Tree of Dreams. They expected to find the grand lady there whose dress was white as new snow trimmed with sunset gold. But their hearts were not pure, and the Dream Tree remained just an oak. Soon they began to sneer at the story. "Hurukay lied to us" they said. "He saw a white woman in disguise."

62

Otsatut, or Wolverine was one of the last to seek the tree. With him he carried an empty jug. Why not a miracle that would keep the jug flowing forever? If the Lady of Dreams had awakened a carved doll, why not a magic bottle? He had heard of such in old folk tales. He told his friends of this and the Christians among them warned him.

"Your wishes are evil, Brother. You may meet with bad luck beneath the tree."

But he ignored them and on a given night, sat beneath the tree and smoked his pipe of clay. As he sat, he thought not of prayer but of the evils the whiteman had brought upon his people when they were powerful. Had the Huron not smote the terrible Iroquois long ago? Our country once covered Ontario and the Great Lakes bear our name. But all is past. Now we live in fear of the Iroquois. And our people have dwindled like windblown ashes."

Wolverine grew angrier. Before the black robes came, we knew only our Manitous, our gods. The missionaries call us pagans and yet our Great Manitou is as powerful as theirs. Even after baptism, the Devil will not go away from some of us they say, but is not the Devil a fallen angel! That is why we say *Otsatut*, or God and the Devil!"

Suddenly the earth began to shake and a rumbling in the forest came toward him. Great trees crashed down, and a heavy body plunged into the water, rending apart the rocks as it fell. Then everything was dreadfully silent.

A flash of light blinded Wolverine. Then in front of him appeared two great eyes blazing with green fire. As his vision cleared he saw the head of the monster, high above the boiling water. It was shaped like that of a horse and when it shook its mane, crackling sparks fell hissing into the river. The scales on the body were of silver and brass while its long body was like a huge snake. It was a serpent, the Great Serpent! Now its wide mouth opened like a cave, its teeth arrow points, its tongue a red spear.

"I hate the Huron Nation," the Serpent roared. "I hate it because it was baptized and I curse it! It shall never grow in size but only grow weaker. But, I love you Wolverine. I am your friend and I bless you!"

Wolverine's teeth were chattering with fear. "But," he pleaded, "Could you make your voice a little softer? I am not deaf and if you stand away a bit, I can see you better. And who are you?"

"I am the guardian spirit of your people, their ancient first master. When I am angry, my voice is *Hinon*, the thunder. It is the lightening that flashes from my eyes, and my breath is the storm. I tear up lakes as I go and dig up rivers. Look at this pit where I fell. It has turned into a waterfall. And the trench beneath is the trail I left when passing."

Again Wolverine pleaded, "Could you please soften your voice?"

"I shall!"

The Serpent then lowered his voice to a whisper, then changed it into the song of a bird. Wolverine's courage began to return. "The black robes," he said, "declare that you, our guardian spirit, and *Le Diable*, the devil, are the same. They say that you capture human souls. It was not you I came to meet, but the White Lady."

"Wolverine, you surprise me. You are not the favorite son of the black-robes though you speak their language, and the Virgin is not your patron saint. Spirit I am, and I hate the Christians, but I love you, and will shower you with blessings. To my friends I am gentle as the rabbit."

"But as a serpent you frighten me."

"As you please," the monster said. I will change you into a toad, a bullfrog or a catfish."

"You are too kind, but let me stay as I was born. Could you become something else less terrible?"

"I can be a bear, a wolf, a lynx, even a rattle snake."

"Can you be a man? Then we can talk."

In an instant the Serpent vanished and in his place stood a dwarf, three feet tall. A wicked smile played about his lips and his eyes were those of the cougar.

"Now listen to what I have to say." said the dwarf.

"Let us talk business," said Wolverine, shrewdly. He was not named Wolverine for nothing but because he was a wily as the *carcajou* itself.

"Pah. You are lazy like the porcupine. You don't work for a living."

"And you are no better than the black robe preachers. *Le Diable* is not as great as I thought." taunted Wolverine.

"We shall see," said the dwarf and tossed a buckskin bag toward the startled Wolverine. "That is filled with gold. Tie it to your belt. It is a witch-purse which never empties no matter how much you spent . . ."

Wolverine's eyes glistened. "My apologies, you are a powerful spirit, M'sieu."

"And something more. Although you have all the clothing you need to cover yourself, you are a vain man and would love to don the satin and plumes of a Seigneur. Here then is the white man's silks, a wampum band for your belt, white wampum for a necklace, silver bracelets and ostrich plumes. You now will look like a chief."

Quickly Wolverine donned the finery and gazed at his image in the river.

"You are also a drunkard," continued the dwarf spirit. Here is the bottle you wished, filled with firewater that will never run dry!"

"*C'est manifique!*" cried Wolverine, happily.

"For all of these things, the black robe wants to throw you from the village. But he does not know who he is dealing with. I will send weasels to his chicken coop, rats in his grain. Every night I will hold a witch's sabbath on his roof with all the black cats for miles around. He will never sleep."

"Aha, that is the best yet," chuckled the Indian. "But what do you want in return for the purse, the clothes and the bottle?"

"The payment is a small thing," said the dwarf.

"A vow to drink myself to death?"

"The same thing, my price is your soul."

"My soul?" Wolverine shuddered.

"Your soul. That is the price."

Wolverine's brow furrowed in thought. "But where will I sleep the first night after my death?"

The dwarf only smiled, then before Wolverine's startled

eyes, he vanished in a cloud of yellow smoke.

Dazed, Wolverine wandered home to sleep. When he awakened, he thought at first it had been a dream, but the bottle, the gold and the clothes lay in a heap on the floor.

From that day on, Wolverine was the richest man in the village. He gave feasts of sagamitte, Indian corn, almost every week in his house. Brandy flowed, the yells and dances of his friends kept half the village awake. The old folks said he had dug up a hidden treasure. No one knew, but now there was much illness in the village. Seeking its cause, they spied at last the Serpent in his hiding place beneath the falls. It was his evil breath that sent the sickness into the village. They called on the curé. What could be done? His answer was that they must exorcise the demon and he announced the same from the pulpit.

The next day, the men gathered with their guns to protect the priest, the women and the children huddled behind closed doors. The men, guns ready, waited at the river brink. Now the priest blessed the water then ordered the serpent to leave. But the serpent hated to leave his fine cave and thrusting out his great head, blinded some of the men with the fumes from his nostrils. Next the priest began reciting prayers from a large book full of ribbons.

At last the serpent could hold out no longer. He crawled from his den, wriggled past the village and headed toward the Straits of Mackinac. On dark nights, it is said, his shining body may be seen near Mackinac Island.

As for Wolverine, no one knows what happened to him. He lived to be an old man, then disappeared. To the devil? Who knows.

THE WITCH'S CAGE

15

After Fort Michilimackinac fell to the British in 1760, the military had several devices to punish soldiers convicted of crimes ranging from drunkeness to desertion. There were stocks, a pillory, a whipping post, a wooden horse which the prisoner was forced to straddle, and a whirligig. The latter consisted of a wooden cage in which the victim could be whirled at great speeds inducing illness or worse. This device was reserved for misbehaving womenfolk.

An old *habitant* and his part Indian grandson were passing the area one day when the old man, Denis Labeau, stopped and pointed to the cage.

"I remember as a boy, seeing a cage in Quebec for prisoners. Only that cage was iron in the shape of human form with hollow arms and legs. At one time a famous prisoner, Marie Josephte Corriveau, was hanged in the cage so that passers by could witness her torture . . ."

"That is strange, *Grand-père*," said the boy. "Tell me about it."

Let us sit on the steps of the trader's house where I can fill my pipe, and I will tell you a tale of the Isle of the Sorcerers."

The boys dark eyes shone. There was nothing he liked better than grandfather's stories, unless they were the Indian Legends told by his Ottawa mother.

The island of which I speak, is called Isle d'Orléans today and lies near Pointe Levis in Quebec. It gained its name because of the strange lights seen there at night, will-o-the-wisps, which lured travelers to their death.

One night a good *habitant* was riding home after an evening with friends. In his dogfish skin bag, he carried a flask of brandy, for it is said that liquor is the milk for old men. His friends had warned him not to leave so late at night, as he would have to pass the cage of La Corriveau. But he only laughed, and rode off. As he passed the cage, he saw the eyeless skull of the wicked creature who was quiet enough, but just in case, he whipped up his horse and raced by. As he passed, he thought he heard a sort of wailing noise, but made up his mind it was only the wind whistling through the bones of the corpse. He halted his horse however, and took a pull at his flask. This somewhat settled his nerves and at the same time he thought to himself, Christians should help the unfortunate and so he removed his cap and recited a *de profundis* for her soul. He then, feeling better, whipped up his horse and headed homeward. But he heard a continuing sound behind him, sort of a tic-tic tic-tic, like iron striking stone. He kept on however, until he reached the high ground of St. Michel. Here drowsiness overtook him, and he decided a short nap might be in order. Dismounting, he hobbled his horse and lay down on the soft grass.

He was about to close his eyes, when a bright light caught his attention. It came from the Isle d'Orléans, and the entire island appeared to be on fire. Leaping to his feet he stared at the strange sight of flames dancing along the shore. It looked as though all the *feu follet*, or will-o-the-whisps from all of Canada, had gathered to hold a witches' sabbath. As his eyes grew accustomed to the light, he realized that the dancers were strange indeed. They had heads as big as a peck measure bearing a yard long pointed cap. Their feet and hands were armed with long claws, and their bodies were those of skeletons. Each had an upper lip split like a rabbits through which protruded a foot long tusk. Their noses were like the snouts of pigs and behind them they dragged long tails twice the length of a cow's.

But strangest of all were their eyes. Some had a single orb

in the middle of their foreheads, others had two eyes, all spurting fire as they whirled round and round like proper Christians doing a dance. Now they began to jump and dance, without moving from their places chanting over and over:

Hoary Frisker, Goblin gay,
Long-nosed neighbor come away!
Come my grumbler in the mud,
Brother Frog of tainted blood!
Come and on this juicy Christian
Let us feast it while we may!

"The accursed heretics," said the old man, shaking his fist. But the hellish chorus struck up yet another song:

Come my trick, traveler's guide,
Devil's minion true and tried,
Come my sucking pig, my Simple.
Brother wart and brother pimple.
Here's a fat and juicy Frenchman
To be pickled, to be fried.

Suddenly the old man saw on the hillside, a mighty devil as tall as the steeple at St. Michel. Instead of the pointed bonnet, he wore a tricorne hat topped with a thorn bush for a feather. He seemed to be the drum major for the regiment for he held a giant saucepan in his hand, twice as big as our 20 gallon maple syrup kettles, and in the other hand a bell clapper which some dog of a heretic had stolen from a church, no doubt. He pounded it on his pan and all the devils began to laugh and jump nodding to the astounded *habitant* as if inviting him to join them.

Now the tall devil began to sing a hellish round, accompanying himself on the saucepan:

Here's the spot that suits us well
When it gets too hot in hell . . .
    Toura-loura,
Here we go all around,
Hands all around,
Here we go all around.

Now the goblins darted in a circle, going completely a-
round the island in less than a minute while the devil sang:

Come along and stir your sticks,
You jolly dogs of heretics,
    Toura-loura.
Room for all, there's room for all
That skim or wriggle, bounce or crawl.
Here we go all around!

The old man began to sweat and great drops rolled down
his forehead and off the tip of his nose. Suddenly behind him,
he heard the same, "tic, tac" which he had heard while on
horseback. But before he could turn around, two great bony
hands, like beasts claws, seized him by the shoulders. He managed to turn his head and gazed straight into the horrible skull-
face of La Corriveau, herself. Now, her arms thrust through
the cage bars, she tried to climb upon his back. But the cage
was heavy and at every leap, she fell backward without losing
her hold. The poor old man was nearly crushed under the
weight and siezed a tree to support himself.

"Now, my dear friend," croaked La Corriveau, "do me the
pleasure of taking me to dance with my friends on the Isle
d'Orléans?"

"You devil's wench!" cried the old man. "Is that the thanks
I get for my prayers? You would drag me into an orgy? I had
thought you must have had three or four thousand years in pur-
gatory for your poisoning pranks. And so I said a *de profundis*
for your black soul. Now you ride me like a heretic!"

But La Corriveau only knocked the cage against the poor
man's head until his skull rattled.

"You hellish wench of Judas Iscariot, I'm not going to be
your jackass and carry you to dance with those mad ones."

"Ho, ho," crowed the witch, "I cannot cross the St. Law-
rence which is a consecrated stream, without the help of a
Christian!"

Suddenly the tall devil stopped beating on his saucepan.
The goblins halted and gave three frightful yells. The island

72

began to shake, wolves, bears and other wild beasts took up the cry.

The old man crossed himself with trembling hands. His time had come!

Now the tall devil struck the pan three times, and there was sudden silence. Stretching out his arm, the devil shouted in a voice of thunder to the poor *habitant* with his ghostly burden: "Make haste, you lazy dog and ferry our friend across. We have only fourteen thousand four hundred more times to dance around the island before cock-crow. Are you going to keep her from the fun?"

"To the devil with all of you," shouted the now enraged habitant. As for you, wench of Satan, would to heaven you still wore the hangman's collar so you wouldn't have so clear a windpipe.

"Very well, croaked the witch." "If your body and soul will not carry me over, I will straddle your soul and ride to the orgy." And with these words she seized him by the throat and he fell senseless to the ground.

"But if he died, Grand-père how could you have learned the story?" asked the boy, wide eyed.

Slowly the old man knocked out his pipe and got to his feet. Then putting his finger alongside his nose, he said, "Because the *old habitant* was me, *mon petit*." And he winked.

SOLDIER GHOSTS

16

Once a long time ago, on Ile Saint Jean (Prince Edward Island), far to the east of Mackinac before the English came, there were many French soldiers camped there. During the French and Indian War many died and a large cemetary was laid out at a place called Port-la Joye, now Charlottetown. After a time the graves were forgotten. The English built a city and one big house was erected right on top of the graves.

When the people moved into the big house, they knew nothing about the cemetary. The house was large, with many rooms and a fine cellar for storing food. But the first night at the stroke of twelve, they heard the sound of a drum from far away. This was followed by the sound of marching men on parade. When the marching stopped there was the bumping of muskets on the ground. Then drums again, and again the marching feet moving off as if after roll call.

The next night the same thing happened. The people couldn't stand the ghostly sounds and moved out. But the next tenant was a hard-headed Scot who didn't believe in ghosts. Still he awakened to the sound of the drums and the marching feet. He didn't mind the sound, his father and his father's father had both been soldiers, but he didn't like the idea of ghosts either.

The next day he made his way to the French part of town and began asking questions. It was then he learned of the cemetary beneath the house.

"Go to the curé," they told him. "He will know what to do."

So the Scot went to the priest and told him of the ghostly noises. The curé shook his head. "Let me come with you to-night to hear the noises." So both set off for a bite of supper, then waited in front of the fireplace for midnight. Again at twelve the ghost company marched to roll call and then off with the drum.

"I will be back," said the curé. "Tomorrow night I will say mass, Monsieur, for those poor fellows who died and were buried without a prayer for their souls. You can help."

The next night he was back. The priest and the Scot went down to the cellar to wait. Above them the clock struck twelve and when the drums sounded, they were ready. As they heard the thump of musket butts as though the company were standing at attention, the priest said the mass and the good Scot read the responses. When the mass was done, the feet marched quickly to the drum and ceased.

From that day forward the Scot lived in peace. The fallen soldiers could lie quiet at last.

HOW THE DEVIL BUILT A CHURCH

17

The Devil, it is said, could change himself into any shape he desired. His favorite was a huge black horse. One day in this disguise, he came to the priest to play a trick. But the priest knew all about him and his ways, and before the horse knew what had happened, the priest had taken his stole from around his neck, and tied it about the neck of the devil horse. The Devil was caught! As long as the stole was tied, it was like holy water and the devil couldn't pass. So now, the great, strong horse, was a prisoner and had to do as the priest bade him.

The father was very pleased and wondered how he could best put the Devil to work for the parish. At last he had it. They would build a fine new church and the horse could pull the stones. Now he would work hard for *le bon Dieu* which should teach him a lesson.

So he harnessed the horse and workmen came from all over the parish to build the church. The black horse strained between the shafts of the French cart without eating or sleeping. "Now he is paying up, thought the curé, for some poor soul he caught like my neighbor, Louis. Maybe he will stay away from our village after this."

So the priest drove the wagon hard, saying prayers in the Devil's laid back ears, blessing the oats so they could not be eaten, sprinkling the straw with holy water so the Devil couldn't sleep, and couldn't even stand still.

The church went up very quickly with the horse hauling stone night and day. The Devil was sick and angry but the stole kept him helpless.

Then one day the priest tied the black horse to a tree and went off to eat *souper*. The Devil horse saw some water in a puddle and tried to reach it, but the stole was too tight. Just then a workman came along and seeing the black horse thirsty, in all kindliness and not knowing it was the Devil, said, "Nice horse, I'll let you have a drink," and he untied the stole.

The great beast reared, made one kick at the church and was out of sight. All that the priest found when he returned, was a smell of sulphur and hoof marks on the stone. But the curé only smiled. The church was finished, and the devil would never return to his parish. And he didn't!

THE DEVIL AND THE GOOD WIFE

18

The voyageurs of Mackinac often told how the Devil had helped build churches, houses and many things. The only problem is, that when it becomes time for the Devil to be paid, the one who hired him may find the price too high.

Once a poor man had to build a new bridge to his farm, but had no money to hire a helper. He had a wife and several children but the boys were too small to lift the heavy timbers. So he did his best, working until late then falling into bed exhausted. One day as he toiled, a stranger stopped to watch. He was a tall man, good black clothes and tricorne hat with plume, with white gloves on his hands.

The farmer paused, doffed his hat thinking the man a *grand seigneur* but the stranger only smiled.

"Do you need help, Monsieur?" he asked politely.

The farmer nodded sadly. "Help I need, but I have no money to pay."

The stranger nodded. "I will help you and next month when I have a heavy job you can work for me. It will cost no money then for you or me."

The farmer was delighted and the tall man took off his fine coat with the silver buttons, but he left on his hat and gloves.

(This was to cover his horns and claws, but the farmer was too happy to think it strange.)

The tall man then held out a paper with writing on it.

85

"This is a contract," said he. "You sign it and we are partners." Then seeing that the farmer could not write, he went on. "Just put a circle here, not a cross, that would spoil the paper . . . " So the farmer made his circle and the bargain was sealed.

The Devil then blew a loud blast through his fingers, and a crew of workmen with a horse came hurrying out of nowhere. The poor farmer couldn't believe his eyes. But the men set to work and he saw the bridge would be ready in another day or two. He was so excited he ran home to tell his good wife.

But when he told her about making a circle on the contract instead of a cross, she was frightened.

"What did the man wear?" she asked, trembling.

"Fine clothes," answered her husband. "All black with white gloves on his hands, like a *Seigneur* from Quebec!"

His poor wife began to cry. "He is not a man from the city. He is the Devil! I have lost you!"

The farmer now turned pale. "What can I do?" he begged.

The good woman wiped away her tears. "I will take care of you, just stay in the house so I can see you at all times."

The terrified farmer didn't stir from his kitchen chair for two days. He couldn't eat, only smoke his *tabac*. On the second evening, the bridge was done so the stranger knocked on the door, then walked into the kitchen, smiling and rubbing his gloved hands.

The wife started to cry, but not like before. "O, don't take him, Monsieur. I have some things to tell him. Say he can just stay a little while!"

The Devil sat down and crossed his legs. "The bridge is finished, the contract is signed and I have other places to go. How much time do you need?"

The good wife hesitated, then suddenly she pointed at a candle half burned down in a saucer. "Let me keep him," she pleaded, "until the candle all burns down."

The Devil gave a great laugh. "That won't take long," said he, "you can keep him sitting in his chair until the candle burns itself out."

But now it was the good wife's time to smile. In an instant

she picked up the candle and blew it out! Then she turned to the stranger. "You don't need to wait, now. That candle will never burn out!"

The Devil leapt to his feet, roaring in anger. But there was nothing he could do but leave.

From that time on the good wife and the lucky farmer kept the candle locked in a closet. And they kept their eyes on it, you can be sure.

THE DEVIL AND THE DANCE

19

During the long winters at Mackinac and at other French settlements, dancing was one of the major forms of entertainment. As today, the prettiest of the girls were the most favored for partners. And the prettiest girl in the village of *Trois Rivieres* far to the east of Mackinac was the miller's daughter, Marie Thérèse. Her hair was crow-wing black, her eyes twin dark moons, her mouth like a red tulip and her voice the murmuring of the river. It must be said, however, that she was perhaps too aware of her beauty. Each night she was reminded of her looks by the coming of the countless young men of the village to her door, bearing gifts of flowers, or ribbons in their nervous hands. And while she hinted to one, Pierre La Framboise, that one day they might marry, she wished to enjoy herself first, to have more money, and to even travel to the city of Quebec for the really big balls and parties. While her father, the miller, was a well-to-do man, he could not afford such fancies and so each night she dreamed of being carried off by a velvet and lace clothed prince to a grand chateau.

One night, the Night of Mardi Gras, which is the last celebration before Lent, Pierre came with his father's sleigh to take Marie to what was always the biggest and best dance of the year. But before she left, her cheeks pink with excitement, her mother said sternly, "Do not forget this is Mardi Gras night. When the clock strikes twelve, you must stop dancing and return home at once or something terrible will happen."

"Do not worry, *chère maman*," answered Marie and off she went with her proud young man. Perhaps, she was thinking, this may be the night my gentleman will come, for people will be there from all over the parish.

It was a grand evening. She danced with all the young men, to the unhappiness of Pierre. Marie had never been happier in her life and forgot her mother's warning until she heard the clock strike twelve. "One more dance," begged Pierre. "One more tune," cried the fiddlers. Marie hesitated, when suddenly the door opened and a stranger came in. Tall, in black clothes, with lace at his throat and sleeves, he was exactly as Marie had dreamed. The stranger stated that it was cold outside, and he begged to rest and get warm. And might he keep on his hat and gloves? Of course all were glad to have so distinguished a visitor and the dance began anew. Then seeing Marie, the stranger bowed and said something nice in her ear. It must have been a request for a dance because she took his gloved hand and they danced around the room. Now he began to talk faster, saying how beautiful she was, why didn't she come to Quebec City and marry a gentleman with money who could give her new clothes and parties the rest of her life?

Pierre watched angrily from the sidelines. Finally he stamped out the door and there he saw the stranger's horse and sleigh, but something was strange. It was a cold night and the snow was deep, but under the black horse's hooves, the snow was melted to the ground.

Suddenly he knew the reason for the stranger's hat and gloves and black clothes. With one bound he was off and running toward the house of the curé. Quickly he told the priest what had happened and the good father put on his coat, took some holy water, and together they ran back to the dance.

As they burst into the room, they saw Marie smiling up into the stranger's face; and heard him say, "Come with me. Give me your hand to seal the contract and we will leave this miserable little village."

She reached out her hand, but as it touched his, she felt the sharp claws beneath his gloves and blood spurted from her tiny palm. Marie turned ashen and fell to the floor in a faint. The stranger bent down to pick her up in his arms, but before he could touch her, the priest leaped between them, dashed holy water on the stricken girl and held up the cross before the stranger.

"She is mine," roared the Devil. "She made a contract in blood!"

But the curé never moved and held the cross steady. Then in solemn tones, he said to the furious Devil, "I have promised her for the convent. You cannot take her ever. Look now at this cross I hold!"

The Devil took one look, howled and disappeared in a cloud of stinking smoke straight through the roof.

The next day, the lovely but sadder Marie Thérèse went to the convent. As for poor Pierre, he left the settlement, joined *Les Compagnies Franches de la Marine* and went into the wild country near Michilimackinac, never to return.

SONGS OF THE VOYAGEURS

20

As the *voyageurs* paddled to and from Mackinac they sang old songs to pass the time and keep the rhythm of their flashing paddles.

One of the oldest of French ballads satirizing the foe of France, William of Orange, became a work song in Canada. Probably unaware of the original political overtones from the Old World, the *voyageurs* found the rhythm ideal to mark the dipping of paddles and to cheer the weary canoemen. The song dates back to the sixteenth century.

> 'Tis the prince of Orange blood
> *Eh La!*
> 'Tis the Prince of Orange blood
> Woke up at the sun's flood
> *Madondaine*
> Arose at the sun's flood.
> *Madondaine.*
>
> Called his page and said,
> "Have you bridled my donkey red?"
>
> "Yes, my prince, 'tis true.
> He's bridled and saddled for you."

To the bridle put his hand,
And feet in stirrup there to stand.

Rode away on Sunday,
Was wounded on the Monday.

Received by grievous change,
Three blows from a long French lance.

In's one leg the first one sank
And two more were in the flank.

Off, while he's yet alive,
And bring a priest for him to shrive.

"What need have I of priest?
I've never sinned I' the least."

"The girls I have never kissed
Unless themselves insist."

"Only a little brunette
And well I've paid my debt."

"Five hundred farthings paid,
And all for a little maid."

This *voyageurs* song, was often heard on the Ottawa River, and in Montreal. The canoemen leaving for the long trip into the wilderness identified with the young lover, for it would be months or perhaps years before they returned to Montreal.

THE LOVER'S FAREWELL

As I was walking through the shade.
I heard my dear beloved weep,
I crept up silently and soft.
Soft and silent as a sleep,
And on her knee my hand I hold,
Saying "Sweetheart, be consoled!"

"A little journey I must take,
'Tis but six months or a year.
"Let your coming home be soon
And you will find me waiting here;
O let your coming home be sped,
That we may crown our eve and wed."

"Sweetheart, come away with me
Until the vessel puts to sea."
When the farewell time is come,
My love and I meet tenderly;
At the time of soft good-byes
Both have tear drops in our eyes.

Only a few French voyageurs were born in France. Yet they sang of their ancestral land.

Few French ports had as much meaning for the first pioneers to sail for the New World, as Saint-Malo. While many forgot the history of the port, the song became a favorite. It tells of the canoeman of three ships that came sailing and was sung often at Michilimackinac around the campfires on the beach.

TO SAINT-MALO

To Saint-Malo, port on the sea,
Did come a sailing vessels three.

> We're going to glide on the water, water, away.
> On the isle, on the isle to play.

Did come sailing vessels fleet
Laden with oats and laden with wheat.

Laden with wheat and laden with oats,
Three ladies came to bargain groats.

Three ladies came in the market street,
"Merchant, tell me the price of wheat."

"Merchant, tell me the price of your grain."
"Three francs for the oats and little to gain."

"Six francs for the wheat, and the oats for three."
And even the half's too dear for me."

"The grain's too dear by more than half."
"If it will not sell, I'll give it like chaff."

"And I'll give it like chaff, if it will not sell,"
"Why then we'll come to terms right well."

96

For 300 years this song was a favorite of the voyageurs, alternating with solo voice and chorus.

EN ROULANT MA BOULE
(A-rolling My Bowl)

Behind our cabin's a little lake,
   A-rolly polely,
   My bowlie rowlie

Two ducks go bathing with a drake
   Rolling my bowl
   For to roll,
   A-rolling my bowl.

Three white feather ducks a-bathing go,
The prince he comes with gun and bow.

The son of the king, the king his son,
He comes to hunt with a silver gun.

With his gun of silver, silver-bright,
Took aim at the black and killed the white.

His aim was black but white the duck,
"O son of the king, you have wicked luck."

"My duck you've killed, my duck was white."
His eyes are a-gleam with diamonds bright.

O from his eyes the diamonds leak,
Gold and silver from his beak.

His beak is dripping golden rings,
And blood is dripping from his wings.

The white duck's wings are dripping blood,
The wind is white with feather-flood.

With all his feathers the wind is thick,
Three ladies gather up and pick.

Three ladies gather the feather yield.
"And we shall make us a bed in the field.

"A feather bed we'll gather and heap.
For two to snuggle, two to sleep.

"We'll sleep on a bed of white duck's feather,
Little children make together,

"Little children will befall,
Children big and children small."

The French Canadian voyageurs and *coureurs des bois* had a remarkable ability to adapt their living to that of the Indians with whom they traded. As Canadian *habitant* clothing wore out, it was replaced by more practical Indian garb. *Mitasses* or leggings of buckskin or brightly colored cloth were worn along with breech clout and loose hunting shirt. Moccasins replaced the buckled shoes and the Indian blankets were turned into hooded coats or *capotes* during winter. Many learned the language and there was much intermarriage. Hence the French Canadians remained friends with the red man even after the English captured Canada. A perfect example was the immunity offered the French during the attack at Michilimackinac by Chippewa warriors in 1763.

The following song is a mixture of French and Indian, probably Huron.

TENAOVICH TENAGA, QUICHKA!*

There came an ancient Indian,
His painted skin was black.
He wore an ancient blanket
And his tobacco sack.
   Quich' -ka' (spoken)
A!, A!, te-na ouich' te-na-ga. Quich' -ka!

He wore an ancient blanket
And his tobacco sack, *Quich' -ka!*
He cried: "Your comrade's dead, sir."
He's dead, alas alack. *Quich' -ka!*

He cried: "Your comrade's dead, Sir!
He's dead, alas alack!;
See there, four ancient braves bear his body on a rack.

"See there, four ancient braves bear his body on a rack.
And two old Swuaws are chanting
In vain to bring him back. *Quich' -ka!*"

*By permission   Gage Educational Publishing Ltd.

The French voyageurs not only sang the old French songs, they composed many as well. The following is reported to be the first Canadian verse written about an actual Canadian incident. It is called *"Petit Rocher"* or "Little Rock." The writer was a trapper named Cadieux and dates back to the early 1700's. Cadieux's poem was found on his dead body, written in blood on a piece of birch bark.

PETIT ROCHER*

As through the forest I cautiously wandered,
Of my dear friends and their fate I pondered.
I asked myself, "Alas have they been drowned?"
"Or by the Iroquois have they all been drowned?"

'Twas just the other day from them I was parted.
And to retrace my pathway I started,
When I saw smoke and feared the worst had come.
For 'twas the Iroquois burning down my home.

I feared the Iroquois in ambush were lying,
So I diverted them, their arrows came flying.
Then I espied three Frenchmen running free:
Great was my joy though I was wounded mortally.

My knees gave way, and my cries were unheeded,
While on their way my friends I had speeded.
Here on this knoll, now friendless and alone,
None will console me or hear my dying moan.

Fly nightingale, to the dear ones I am leaving.
Fly to my wife and my little ones grieving
Tell them I guarded love and loyalty,
And to abandon any hope of seeing me.

Here, thus abandoned, I lie unrelenting; And in the
    Saviour I have faith, unrelenting.
Oh, Holy Virgin, unfold your arms to me,
There would I lie for all eternity.

*By permission   Gage Educational Publishing Ltd.

The End...

ABOUT THE AUTHOR - ARTIST

Dirk Gringhuis was born in Grand Rapids, Michigan. Since 1947, he has written and illustrated 28 books for young people, many dealing with Michigan's early history, its pioneers, Indians and soliders. Among them are *The Great Parade*, Tall tales and true of Michigan's past; *The Young Voyageur*, Fort Michilimackinac and Pontiac's war; *Were-Wolves and Will-o-the-Wisps*, voyageur's folk tales at Mackinac; *Let's Color Michigan*, *Lore of the Great Turtle* and others. He is author-illustrator also of *In Grey-White and Blue, French Troops at Mackinac 1715-1760*; and *Indian Costume at Mackinac*, published by the Mackinac Island State Commission in their Mackinac History series.

In addition to his books, Gringhuis was Producer-Host for a weekly series on Educational television for nine years.

As an historical muralist, he painted over 15 murals for Forts Mackinac and Michilimackinac as well as drawings for the Indian Dormitory on Mackinac Island and the French Trader's House at Michilimackinac.

He was given special awards for his work on Michigan including the Governor's Award, a Merit Award from the Michigan Historical Society, and a national Educational Television Award. He is listed in Who's Who in the Midwest.

Gringhuis lived with his wife in East Lansing, Michigan and was curator of Exhibits for the Museum at Michigan State University as well as Associate Professor in Elementary Education.

This is Dirk Gringhuis' last book. He died while *Were-Wolves and Will-o-the-Wisps* was being printed. His good humor, vivid stories and lively drawings will be missed by many. Yet his books and art lives on.

102

CONSULTANTS AND SOURCES

Special thanks to the following individuals for their invaluable assistance in the preparation of this book. Dr. Roxane C. Carlisle, Head of the Ethnomusicology Section and Renée Landry, Assistant Archivist, Canadian Centre for Folk Culture Studies, National Museum of Man, Ottawa, Ontario. René Chartrand, Curator, National Historic Sites, Ottawa, Ontario. Brian L. Dunnigan, Assistant Curator, Mackinac Island State Park Commission. The National Archives and National Library, Ottawa, Ontario. The Michigan State University Library, East Lansing, Michigan.

The following sources provided the stories and songs herein retold. Honoré Beaugrand, *New Studies of Canadian Folk Lore* (1904); Philippe Aubert de Gaspé, *The Canadians of Old* (1890); Marie Caroline Hamlin, *Legends of Le Detroit* (1894); The Works of Charles Marius Barbeau; Gage Educational Publishing Ltd., Agincourt, Ontario.

This research and writing of this work was made possible by an all-university grant by Michigan State University.

INDEX

The Forts of Mackinac
Guide to official publications
Mackinac Island State Park Commission

Mackinac Island — Its History in Pictures
Over 360 historic photographs and drawings lavishly presented, depict the fascinating history of Mackinac Island.

France at Mackinac
The fascinating story of French architecture, clothing, food and life as told in eighteenth century pictures and artifacts . . . 44 pages.

Gentlemen on the Frontier
Photographs of the findings of Michilimackinac's archaeologists, words of the fort's inhabitants, and eighteenth-century woodcuts reveal life in Fort Michilimackinac . . . 68 pages with 1,100 artifacts.

The Doctor's Secret Journal
Frank revelations, amusing, shocking, but always fascinating, by Fort Michilimackinac's surgeon's mate 1769-1772 . . . 47 pages.

Attack at Michilimackinac — 1763
The harrowing adventures of Alexander Henry, an eyewitness to the bloody Indian massacre at Fort Michilimackinac . . . 126 pages.

Treason? at Michilimackinac
The vision and sufferings of Robert Rogers as recorded in the official transcript of his trial for treason in 1768 . . . 103 pages.

Soldiers of Mackinac Set A   4 prints
Color prints suitable for framing of the 60th Regiment 1763, The King's Eighth 1775, Wayne's Legion 1796 and 1st Regiment of Artillery 1812.

Soldiers of Mackinac Set B   4 prints
Mackinac Militiaman 1752, Chippewa Warrior 1763, 10th Royal Veteran 1812, and 10th Infantry 1882.

Preservation of History at Mackinac
Report of the innovative program of historic preservation and reconstruction at Fort Michilimackinac and Mackinac Island. Profusely illustrated . . . 47 pages.

War 1812
The exciting history of how the British, Indians, and Americans fought for Mackinac Island from 1812 to 1815 . . . 43 pages.

Historic Guidebook, Mackinac Island
A description of points of historic and scenic interest on Mackinac Island, with maps and suggested walking tours . . . 41 pages.

The Young Voyageur
For the young readers — A gripping historical novel about trade and treachery at Michilimackinac in 1763 . . . 202 pages.

Lore of the Great Turtle
Indian Legends of Mackinac retold and lavishly illustrated . . . 96 pages.

Were-Wolves and Will-O-The Wisps
French legends of Mackinac retold and richly illustrated . . . 106 pages.

18th Century Military Buttons
Recastings in pewter from original buttons excavated at Fort Michilimackinac and Fort Mackinac.

Mackinac History Volume I
Twelve illustrated vignettes about the life and culture of Michilimackinac and Mackinac Island.

Indian Costume at Mackinac
Indian costume during the seventeenth and eighteenth centuries illustrated in color . . . 12 pages.

Reveille Till Taps
Soldier life at Fort Mackinac, 1780-1895, told in words and pictures . . . 116 pages.

Marquette Mission Site
Archaeological excavation at the site of Father Marquette's mission in St. Ignace . . . 35 pages.

King's Men at Mackinac
Sixteen British units 1780-1796 described and illustrated in full color . . . 38 pages.

Mackinac Island State Park Commission
Mackinac Island, Michigan 49757